dream big!

McKay
and the
Magical
Hat

Kate David

Illustrated by:

Helen Turner

Outskirts Press, Inc.
http://www.outskirtspress.com

ISBN: 978-1-4787-2968-6

Outskirts Press and the "OP" logo are trademarks belonging to Outskirts Press, Inc.

PRINTED IN THE UNITED STATES OF AMERICA

To my sweet McKay,
whose imagination inspires me.
-Kate

For Luke,
who makes me smile everyday.
-Helen

McKay stood next to her big sister Murphy with a puzzled look on her face.

"My friend Tommy said he's going to be the President when he grows up. What do you think I can be?" McKay asked.

"It's what YOU want to be that matters, McKay! But before you decide, let's imagine all the possibilities!"

"I want to be
a Firefighter!"
McKay announced.

"I want to be a
Super Hero!"
Murphy added.

"Let's get the magical
hat!" Murphy said.

"We can be anything we want to
be when we put it on!" She added,
as the girls raced upstairs and into their
Mother's bedroom.

They reached into the trunk at the foot of the bed and pulled out the magical hat.

"You put it on, McKay! It's your turn for an adventure!"

McKay climbed onto her Mother's bed and began to think about all the things she could be when she grew up. She placed the magical hat on her head, closed her eyes tightly and when she opened them...

McKay spun around the room with a twirl.
Her dancing dreams rushed in with a whirl.

Practicing along the mirror-covered wall,
she heard thunderous applause for her curtain call.

I could be a Ballerina leaping in my Pointe shoes,
dancing as the lights catch my tutu's pink hues.

She closed her eyes again and when she opened them wide,
a large stack of pancakes was piled at her side.

McKay stood prepping and mixing dishes to bake
and then focused on decorating a beautiful cake.

The stove held several bubbling pots and pans,
as she kneaded the dough with her own two hands.

I could be a Chef, making the kitchen a mess.
I could own a restaurant and enjoy its success.

As she thought about the dreams of her future,
she checked on a little boy who needed a suture.

McKay was wearing a white doctor's coat
and used her equipment to check his ears and throat.

With the black stethoscope hung around her neck,
she listened to his heart for one final check.

I could be a Doctor helping a child in pain.
No broken bones today, it's just a sprain.

Seeing her future looking so bright,
McKay was teaching a child to read and write.

As she recited the alphabet written in chalk,
her students then studied the numbers on a clock.

She sat with a student to sound out a word
and explained that letters are sometimes seen but not heard.

I could be a Teacher, helping
children eager to learn.
We could all celebrate the grades
they worked hard to earn.

One final time, her eyes
opened and closed.
Now, she sat at a desk with
the blueprints proposed.

McKay held the sketches wide in her hands,
as she carefully reviewed the construction plans.

The design of the building was hers to create.
Her artistic skills were an inherited trait.

I could be an Architect designing a dream home.
With that, McKay's imagination continued to roam.

A Scientist in a coat so white.

A Pilot ready to take a flight.

A Florist creating a beautiful bouquet.

A Pastry Chef baking
a chocolate soufflé.

A Contractor who wears
a yellow hard hat.

A Veterinarian soothing a sick cat.

An Athlete lacing her shoe.

An Officer in a uniform of blue.

A Rock Star singing a favorite tune.

An Astronaut soaring
off to the Moon.

An Artist using a
paint soaked brush.

A Mother swaying and whispering hush.

McKay lifted the magical hat off her head and opened her big blue eyes.

She felt the feathery pillow behind her and instantly knew that she was back home.

"What did you decide to be when you grow up?" Murphy asked.

McKay answered with delight, "I don't know yet, but I know I can be anything I imagine!"

CPSIA information can be obtained
at www.ICGtesting.com
Printed in the USA
LVIC06n1000181214
418062LV00002BA/2